Myrtle the Turtle Discovers Hug Power

Jan DiSanto

Myrtle the Turtle Discovers Hug Power

iUniverse books may be ordered through booksellers or by contacting:

iUniverse
1663 Liberty Drive
Bloomington, IN 47403
www.iuniverse.com
1-800-Authors (1-800-288-4677)

ISBN: 978-1-5320-3608-8 (sc)
ISBN: 978-1-5320-3609-5 (e)
ISBN: 978-1-5320-3610-1 (hc)

Library of Congress Control Number: 2017916551

Print information available on the last page.

iUniverse rev. date: 02/15/2018

This engaging and inspiring book belongs to:

This book is dedicated to the young girl who inspired it. It is also dedicated to all of us who strive to heal our shame and develop a secure connection with others, and to those who help with this process.

Once upon a time, on an island in the great Pacific Ocean, there lived a tiny sea turtle named Myrtle. Myrtle was the youngest and smallest of all the turtles in her family. There was Mama Turtle; Big Daddy Turtle; Myrtle's brother, Yertle; and lots of cousins.

The cousins were Nerdle, Flirtle, Squirtle, Blurtle, and Fertile. Nerdle the Turtle was smart and knew all the names of the different types of coral and sea creatures. Flirtle the Turtle was cute and knew it. Squirtle the Turtle wasn't yet toilet-trained. Blurtle the Turtle couldn't stop herself from saying things that shouldn't be said. Lastly, there was Fertile Turtle, who always laid more eggs than the other turtles.

Myrtle was a happy little turtle and liked being the youngest, *except* at certain times. One of those times was when she was jealous of her big brother, Yertle. He could swim faster than she could; he could go places she couldn't go; and he understood things that she didn't—like funny things her parents said. It was like they were all in a club that Myrtle didn't belong to.

Yertle could go off with his turtle friends and explore the other side of the reef, while Myrtle had to stay in the sheltered lagoon. He could go where the water was deep and exciting things happened—like pods of dolphins coming by, and big beautiful fish, and even whales!

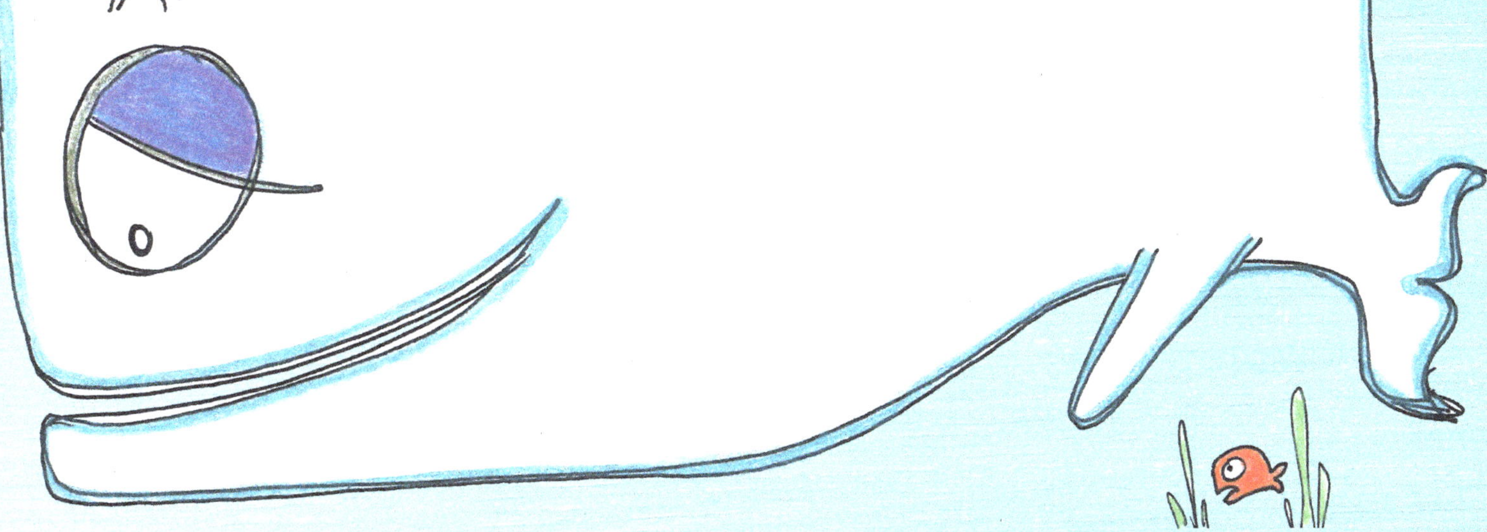

When she was jealous, Myrtle didn't realize that when her brother was little, *he* couldn't do those things either. She didn't realize that *she* would be able to do those things and more when she got older. Myrtle felt like that was just too long to wait. She was impatient.

One day when Yertle came back and was telling the family about his adventures, Myrtle began to really want to go off and explore too. So she sneaked away and began swimming across the reef toward the back side, where the water was deep.

Suddenly, Myrtle began to get the "uh-oh" feeling in her stomach. It was the kind of feeling that happens when we are doing something we know we shouldn't do. It didn't feel good to Myrtle, but she decided not to pay attention to it.

Myrtle swam and swam. She went through some thick seaweed and past lots of spiky sea urchins and colorful fish.

Meanwhile, Mama Turtle and Big Daddy Turtle realized Myrtle was gone, and they were scared. They began to call out for her and search for her, swimming in all directions. They called and swam and called and swam.

Finally, they caught up to Myrtle. Big Daddy took his big flipper and scooped her up. Mama scolded her: "You know you're not supposed to go outside the lagoon!"

Myrtle was mortified! She did not like being scolded. She felt bad. She felt like she *was* bad.

When they got back inside the lagoon, Myrtle felt so horrible that she wanted to hide. She knew she had made a mistake. Myrtle knew better than to go off by herself into the deep water. She had ignored the "uh-oh" feeling and done it anyway.

What she didn't know was that everyone made mistakes. She didn't know that her brother made mistakes and that was how he learned. Even Mama and Big Daddy made mistakes—even big ones sometimes!

Myrtle felt so bad that she held her breath, sank to the bottom behind a big rock, and cried. She was very embarrassed about making a mistake and about being scolded.

But then she got *MAD*. When she was ashamed, she got mad at herself. When she was mad at herself, she got mad at everyone else!

Now, turtles can only hold their breath for a certain amount of time. When Myrtle came up for air, there was Mama Turtle. Myrtle started to scream and snap at Mama Turtle, but Mama Turtle saw that Myrtle was upset and knew what was going on.

She scooped the little turtle up with her flippers and said, "Let me tell you a story, Myrtle." Myrtle fought for a few moments but could feel Mama's love for her, so she settled down and listened to the story.

"A long time ago, before you were born, you were a spirit just like all living things—a beautiful spark of light, like a star twinkling in the night. When you were born, you were pure and innocent, and your heart was full of love. All of this is still true. Your spirit is pure and innocent and full of love, even if you make a mistake.

"But when turtle spirits hatch and become turtles, they forget about this. When something bad happens, they begin to feel bad about themselves. So they go from feeling all good to feeling very bad. Then they can even decide that they *are* bad."

Mama Turtle said to Myrtle, "Now let me tell you how this happens. We all have a little voice in our heads that sometimes tells us bad things. When it says bad things, it can turn into a monster. The more bad things you believe, the bigger it gets. Sometimes it can look like this:

"It's the shame monster. You can make it grow or shrink. The more you believe the bad things it says, the more the shame monster grows. But the more you know that your spirit is full of love and you let yourself be comforted by the love and connection from your family, the more it shrinks."

Mama Turtle continued, "The best way to get it to shrink when you have the bad feeling is to tell me that the shame monster is paying you a visit, and I will give you a big hug. Hugs can help melt the shame monster. They can also help you remember the beautiful spark of light inside you that is love."

Just then, Myrtle asked her mother for a hug. When Mama Turtle hugged her, she began to feel a bit better. She could feel Mama's love for her, and she could feel the shame monster shrink. The more she let herself feel that love, the better she felt.

Myrtle then swam off to play with her cousins. Later that day, she noticed the bad feeling was gone! She thought about the hug from her mother. She could feel Mama Turtle's love for her and how that helped her feel better. *Wow!* she thought. She was learning something new.

She joined her cousins and began playing hide-and-seek. They were all having lots of fun. But then Myrtle noticed that they were going farther and farther out toward the edge of the lagoon, close to the deep water. She began to get the "uh-oh" feeling.

She called to her friends and gathered them up.

"I don't think we ought to go out any farther," Myrtle told them.

"Don't be such a baby," said Blurtle.

"You're no fun," said Flirtle.

"Well, we could get into trouble," said Fertile.

Myrtle felt bad that Blurtle and Flirtle didn't want to listen to her and said things to her that weren't nice. She remembered what had happened the last time she ignored the "uh-oh" feeling and how that left her feeling bad. She also thought about Mama's hug and how good that made her feel. So she said to her friends, "You can do what you want, but I'm staying here."

"I'll stay with you," said Fertile.

Myrtle and Fertile continued playing in the lagoon and having fun while Blurtle and Flirtle went farther out into the deep water.

Myrtle still had the "uh-oh" feeling, but not for herself. She had it for her cousins, but she knew they might have to learn for themselves.

When they were done playing, Myrtle swam back to her parents. They were happy to see her, and she was happy to see them.

That night at bedtime, Myrtle asked her parents, "If I feel bad again, will you give me a hug?"

They said, "Of course!"

She felt good about that and asked for a hug right then and there.

Myrtle had discovered HUG POWER!

The End

On separate pieces of paper:

Draw a picture of what your shame monster looks like.

Now, draw a picture of what your spirit energy looks like.

Finally, draw a picture of your shame monster shrinking.

Possible Discussion Questions to Use with Children

The following questions can be used to facilitate a discussion with children after reading the book. Some of these questions may be more useful than others with a certain child at certain times. Not all children will be open to discussing the book or answering questions, so it's important to be respectful of and sensitive to the child's needs. These questions can help integrate the concepts in the book by promoting self-awareness and can open a new dialogue between parent and child.

Have you ever had the "uh-oh" feeling?

Where do you feel that in your body? What does it feel like?

Do you sometimes pay attention to it and sometimes not?

What do you usually do when you get the "uh-oh" feeling?

What happens when you do pay attention to it?

What happens when you don't pay attention to it?

Have you ever felt bad like Myrtle and wanted to hide?

Do you hide, or do you do something else?

Do you think you could ask Mom or Dad for a hug if you feel bad like Myrtle?

Do you ever feel bad inside yourself and then get angry?

What does that feel like in your body?

What do you do when you get angry?

Do you think Myrtle learned something?

What do you think she learned?

Note to Parents and Other Readers

I was inspired to write this book after watching a five-year-old child I know go through a significant experience of shame when very mildly corrected by her mother. She withdrew from the gathering, isolating herself on an outside deck. When her mother came to talk to her, the child first berated herself and then lashed out in anger at her mother. They were out on the deck for a prolonged period of time.

Eventually they came inside, and a teenage cousin distracted the child, who began playing and let go of the shame. When I witnessed all of this unfolding, I saw that the resolution of the shame was not complete. I had the thought that perhaps a therapeutic story could help her. This story came to me. I chose to write about a turtle because that was the favorite animal of this little girl.

It's impossible for a child to get through childhood without some sort of incident that could engender shame. For that matter, a large percentage of adults are carrying shame from their childhoods. I decided to write a story that would speak to this universal experience and be beneficial for both children and the adults who care for them and read stories to them.

When shame is triggered, the typical responses are as follows:

withdraw, deny (acting shameless)
attack oneself (becoming self-critical, perfectionistic)
attack others (with blaming or anger)

One or all of these behaviors might be engaged in. In the real-life situation with this five-year-old, I saw the withdrawal and collapse, the attacking of herself, and the attacking of another (her mother). I have constructed my story along these lines.

First, an incident happens that triggers shame, then there is withdrawal, and then attacking of self and others. This shaming–blaming is a defense. In the real-life situation that I witnessed, the resolution of the shame wasn't complete, as the child would not let herself be soothed by her mother. She only got out of the shame when she was distracted—not by allowing herself to be comforted by her mother. This was a fairly common pattern with this child.

The theorists who write about shame call withdrawal the "breaking of the interpersonal bridge,"[1] because people in shame pull in toward themselves and isolate themselves from others. The interpersonal bridge is the connection to others. There are two types of shame: healthy shame and toxic shame.

[1] Gershen Kaufman, *The Psychology of Shame: Theory and Treatment of Shame-Based Syndromes* (New York: Springer, 2004), 33.

Healthy shame comes when people do something wrong that violates either their internal moral code or the social code of their society, and they feel appropriately bad about it. This type of shame is designed to prevent us from being harmed or even killed, and it helps us stay in the human community. It is a major socialization tool.

Toxic shame comes when people feel they are bad, flawed, or defective. When this occurs, there is a sudden interruption of pleasure and a shutdown or freeze state in the body. These people want to run away and hide. They don't want anyone's eyes on them. This is a protective response that is wired into our nervous systems. It is set up to protect us from doing something dangerous to ourselves or our tribe. The body goes into shutdown. It's a very painful state.

In the book, Myrtle gets the "uh-oh" feeling, which is a signal that she is doing something she knows she should not do. This is intended to help children begin to pay attention when they get that feeling, so they can interpret it and listen to it.

This book is primarily about repairing shame when it happens. The first step in repairing shame is when Mama Turtle comes and reconnects with Myrtle. Mama sees that Myrtle is in a state of toxic shame. Myrtle feels she is bad, not simply that she did something wrong. That's when she sinks to the bottom and hides.

Mama reaches out to help her, and even though Myrtle initially fights her, Mama doesn't give up. She stays with Myrtle and tries to connect with her daughter by addressing Myrtle's feelings, talking about the shame monster, and telling a story. One of the ways to work with shame is to name it and externalize it. That's why the shame monster is brought into the story.

The shame monster is an externalization of the feeling of shame. It brings the shame outside the person, separating the shame from the person's essential self and allowing the individual to dis-identify with it. It frames shame as something that is happening *to* the person—the shame monster is paying you a visit—rather than something that is inherent *in* the person.

Mama Turtle also cleverly tells Myrtle a story about being a pure and innocent spirit when she was born. This helps Myrtle reconnect with her basic goodness. It gives her the message that Mama Turtle does not see her as bad. This is a corrective emotional experience. Mama Turtle also gives Myrtle a way to melt the shame monster by telling her that the shame monster is paying her a visit and that a hug will help melt the monster. Then Mama offers her a hug.

A powerful antidote to shame is to be seen as good and worthy by someone who cares about you. It helps to know that this person doesn't see you as bad, flawed, or defective and to feel connected. This is the repairing of the interpersonal bridge.

Myrtle notices that she feels better after the hug, which is a sign that the antidote is working. On a biological level, feeling safe and loved can activate the release of oxytocin, the hormone of calmness, connection, safety, and trust. It acts as an immediate antidote to cortisol, the stress hormone. It stops the response of fight-flight-freeze. Hugs are particularly effective at releasing oxytocin.

The last part of the story has Myrtle playing with her friends and having an opportunity to utilize what she just learned. When she gets the "uh-oh" feeling a second time, she pays attention to it and has the strength to do what she knows is right. Her recent positive interaction with Mama Turtle helps her to do that.

At the end of the story, Myrtle is able to reflect on her experience by asking Mama, "If I feel bad again, will you give me a hug?" That is how she discovers hug power.

After this ending, I included a suggestion for children to draw pictures of their shame monster, their spirit energy, and the shame monster shrinking on separate pieces of paper. This is intended to be an experiential exercise that engages the child psychologically and emotionally in a self-reflective way and deepens the message and impact of the book. In doing this, children are more likely to apply the concepts to themselves. This is something they can do once again after subsequent readings.

I would also encourage parents to draw pictures for themselves along with their child, if they are so inclined. Drawing three pictures in this sequence utilizes a technique for processing emotional material called *pendulation*.[2] In pendulation, you move easily from one sensation, feeling, thought, or visual image to another. This helps to soften and discharge the difficult experience—in this case shame—and to relax the nervous system so that the person can move in a more life-affirming direction. The shame gets repaired with a new awareness of the self.

Pendulation also gives people a tool to work with shame should it come up in the future. They will have visual images in their minds that represent the goodness of their beings. The more we repeat this, the more it can dissolve the shame.

Several months after I gave the book to the little girl who inspired it, I heard from her mother that when she has an upsetting incident that triggers her into anger or shame, she now says, "That's not me. It's the shame monster! Let's shrink the shame monster!" They then engage in a ritual of shrinking the shame monster and utilizing hug power to facilitate her in moving out of this dysregulated state.

---

[2] Peter Levine, *Healing Trauma: A Pioneering Program for Restoring the Wisdom of Your Body* (Boulder, Colorado: Sounds True, 2005), 56-8.

About the Author

Jan DiSanto, RN, MS, MFT, has been a licensed psychotherapist for more than forty years and is currently in private practice in California. She is an Emotionally Focused Couples Therapist and supervisor and is trained in EMDR, IFS, and hypnosis. Attachment and shame have been a personal and professional focus throughout her career working with individuals, couples, families, and children.

Jan lives in Mill Valley, California, with her husband, Peter. They have two grown children and, so far, one grandchild. Her daughter, Lani Yadegar, did the illustrations for this book. Jan can be contacted at myrtletheturtlebook@gmail.com, and the website is www.MyrtletheTurtlebook.com.

Jan is pleased to have written a lighthearted book on this important subject that can contribute to an understanding of shame and also benefit parents and anyone who works with or cares for children. She hopes this book will be helpful and healing for children, as well as for the adults we have already become.

About the Illustrator

Lani Yadegar is a relationship coach and artist. She has been doodling pictures of sea creatures for more than twenty-five years, since she was a little one playing on the beaches of Hawaii. She lives in Lagunitas, California, with her husband, Dave; her daughter, Zoë Valentina (a.k.a. ZoZo Bear); and her dog, Zahla Puppy. Her shame monster is still shrinking, but it is a lot smaller than it used to be, and she likes lots of hugs.

Lani has always loved children's books and is happy to be able to put all those years of sea creature doodling to good use! She can be contacted at lani.yadegar@gmail.com.

In this book, the main character, Myrtle the Turtle, is jealous of her older brother. She decides to go off exploring on her own, as he is able to, even though she is considered too young to do so by her parents. She ignores a warning from inside herself (the "uh-oh" feeling) that she should not do this.

Her parents are alarmed that she is gone, and when they find her, they scold her. First Myrtle feels ashamed, and then feels she is bad, and so she hides. When Mama Turtle finds her, Myrtle gets angry.

Mama Turtle is wise and understands what is going on. She addresses Myrtle's emotional state sensitively and creatively. Mama stays connected to Myrtle, tells her a story that is countershaming, and hugs her. That reestablishes their connection, which is an antidote to shame. Myrtle begins to feel better and stronger within herself and is then able to utilize what she learned with her friends and herself.

This is a disarming book that helps children and parents deal with naturally occurring shame and promotes the connection between parent and child. Myrtle the Turtle disobeys her parents and goes off on her own. When scolded, Myrtle falls into shame and anger. Her mother helps her resolve these feelings through their loving bond. As a result, Myrtle learns from the experience and feels stronger within herself.

Finally! A children's book about shame—that universal, powerful, and misunderstood emotion. Brilliantly written and delightfully drawn, *Myrtle the Turtle Discovers Hug Power* explores the inner emotional world of the child. Jealousy, impatience, and the reactions to shame are gently and humorously explored in this fanciful tale, leading to a happy ending as Myrtle's shame is healed. Recommended for parents, teachers, therapists, and kids of all ages.

-Sheila Rubin, LMFT, and Bret Lyon, PhD
Co-creators of the Healing Shame workshops

Jan DiSanto has very cleverly disguised a wise book for adults in the form of a children's book. It teaches parents how to help their children not carry around the burden of shame while entertaining the children with a comforting story that can be appreciated on many levels. It is a truly engaging story that both parents and children will gain from reading. The author is a sophisticated, emotionally focused therapist, and it shows. The drawings (by Jan's daughter!) convey just the right amount of emotion to fit the story. Bravo to them both!

—Hanna Levenson, PhD, psychologist
Professor, Wright Institute.

Jan DiSanto has written a lively and clever book for young children, playfully illustrated, about how young Myrtle the Turtle experiences shame, learns to listen to her inner voice, and connects with loved ones. It relays the message that we all experience shame and that healing can take place through connection in loving relationships. Most helpful is the included guide parents can use to dialogue with their children about these experiences. It is an important addition to a child's library that will enhance learning with every rereading.

—Liza J. Ravitz, PhD
Child and adult psychologist and Jungian analyst

This is a refreshing and pragmatic book addressing the feelings of shame in children. Ms. DiSanto integrates a wonderful set of illustrations with a text that is clear and easy to use. I highly recommend it as a teaching tool for parents and other adults involved in child-rearing.

—Ian A. Canino, MD
Clinical professor emeritus of child psychiatry, Columbia University

CPSIA information can be obtained
at www.ICGtesting.com
Printed in the USA
BVHW02s0305160418
513370BV00017B/127/P

9 781532 036088